THE PARIS STORIES

LIBRARY OF CONGRESS CATALOGUING IN PUBLICATION DATA

Hunt, Laird
The Paris Stories.
Prose in English
ISBN: 978-1-934851-21-0
Copyright © by Marick Press, 2010
Design and typesetting by Alison Carr
Cover design by Marick Press
Cover image: Kathryn Hunt.
Acknowledgements to
Smokeproof Press who first published The Paris Stories in 2000.
Printed and bound in the United States
Marick Press
P.O. Box 36253
Grosse Pointe Farms
Michigan 48236
www.marickpress.com
Distributed by spdbooks.org
And Ingram

The text at the top of page 95 is by Robert Walser and was translated from
the German by Shawn Huelle.

THE PARIS STORIES

(small sicknesses of love)

LAIRD HUNT

MARICK PRESS

De cent membres et visages qu'a chaque chose, j'en prens un...
J'y donne une poincte, non pas plus largement, mais
le plus profondement que je sçay...Sans dessein, sans promesse,
je ne suis pas tenu d'en faire bon, ny de m'y tenir moy mesme,
sans varier quand it me plaist, et me rendre au doubte et a
l'incertitude, et a ma maitresse forme qui est l'ignorance.

—Michel de Montaigne

SMALL SICKNESSES OF LOVE

I

Dear Sweetheart,

On a sunny day in Paris you can observe shadow engaged in all shape and variety of exotica. Example: two long shadows, in the center of an immense and imbricate field of waving shadow, on either side of one short, squat, fixed shadow, unwrapping what you then look up and see are ice cream cones.

II

In 14th century Occitan (as reported by Jacques Fournier, Bishop of Pames, future Pope at Avignon), in a village called Montaillou, the 250 odd citizens (or heretics as Fournier had—too often literally—branded them) lived in envelopes of perceived space and time so small that by closing their eyes and making cross bars of their arms they could slip straight out of the spacio-temporal and finger the Divine.

This Divine, as most immediately if perhaps inaccurately personified by Fournier and his hot-poker and yellow-badge wielding Inquisition, was both ticklish and ill-tempered.

One swung one's arms carefully and guarded against the incipient iniquity
of closing one's eyes.

III

Years ago, before Paris, before this Paris, mine, I sat in a dark room with 10
or 12 others and watched as an old projector poured light onto a screen.

That was Physics.

Hands spilled liquids from glass to glass and we saw viscosity.
Water rushed through turbines and cities turned on.
There was the dark granite steeple.
And there was the star.
The star's name was The Sun.

IV

I walked through the Musée de L'homme stopping here in front of the
Instruments of the World Display, and then here in front of the Skull Display
(4 grey skulls sitting on a shelf), then here in front of the Overpopulation
of the World Display, and then here in the center of the Bridge of Infinity
Display, where I opened my arms.
Which didn't accomplish much.
Once I asked a very small kid friend I had what she thought happened to her
skeleton when she slept, and her answer was: Gravity.

Cars go by in the distance.
Everything goes by in the distance.

There is this anecdote I'm very much attached to about the trip Flaubert
took to Egypt with Maxime du Camp in which du Camp spent the whole
trip trying out his new-fangled photographic apparatus and Flaubert spent
the whole time dozing on the boat.

I sleep too much.

Once a friend, albeit politely, complained about it. She said that maybe
the next day, given that we were in Paris, and it was reportedly lovely, we
could spend outside. I said something half-baked about the necessity of
elaborating my relationship to the Orphic underworld.
She said that maybe the next day *she* would spend outside.

V

I associate, rightly or wrongly, my impending dissolution, with the
dissolution, in my body, of time.

In this section of the Catalogue leaves beat against the window glass and I
don't sleep.

Dear Sweetheart,

VI

In writing on medieval culture J. Le Goff speaks of an 'immense appetite for the Divine'. In going through my writings I came across this:

My Father illustrating the mechanisms of orbit.

His fist, Sun. A plum, Earth.

—And what about the Moon.

Fist. Plum. Fist.

We rose.

I understood the connective forces to be filament.

Clear.

—Like fishing line.

I could see it.

My fist shook.

Which runs, in combination with Le Goff's descriptive axiom, as a useful tangent to the following which I once (and you can believe I was jealous) overheard a young woman whispering to a young man on the metro:

"I wish I could kiss your bones."

VII

In *The Hours of Catherine of Cleves*, a 15th century illuminated devotional, you can find a picture of Adam's bones lying in a tiny white pile at the base of a tree.

Dear Adam,

Orpheus had only his voice and lyre and walked almost out of hell with a jeweled shadow. Flaubert had only his pen and dozings and walked out of the 19th century with Paris. I walked out of my apartment and it was late Spring. Water was running in the gutters. People were sitting on the terraces. Someone, somewhere, was playing music. Couples were walking together along the street. I said something about the light playing off the water and onto the wall and a guy, some old guy I'd never seen before, stopped.
Yeah he said.
I pointed.
Shhh, he said. And walked off.

VIII

There is a commercial running on the movie screens of Paris that shows an elephant swimming through blue water. The blue water is in a bay surrounded by white cliffs and in the center of the bay is a young woman reading on a raft under a yellow umbrella beside two bottles of Coca Cola on ice. The elephant is filmed from the side then from below. The elephant is swimming towards the raft. The woman is very tan and everything outside the water with the exception of the Coca Cola on ice looks hot. There is a lazy-summer-day music playing so we know that the goal of the elephant swimming towards the raft is a happy one. It is not possible to see what book the woman is reading though it's almost possible—for about half a second— to see her eyes. It is possible, however, to see the elephant's trunk: long, sinuous, strangely delicate, wet. The trunk silently deposits three water-soaked peanuts on the raft then wraps itself around one of the bottles of Coke. Then, Coke in trunk, the elephant swims off and music, woman, raft, blue water, white cliffs, yellow umbrella, Coke, ice, and elephant fade.

In *The Day the Earth Stood Still* the earth does not really stand still but for half an hour all engines and electricity stop. The people, however, do not stop, and for a moment, as I sat in the theater and watched them move through the maze of frozen cars, darkened hallways, and silent streets, I was awed.

Joyce called Paris "The last of the human cities."

On a slim white column in "The last of the human cities" a young woman once projected the image of a hand pulling a stick through sand. I dreamed about it afterwards and in the dream the hand moving around and around the column was moving around and around my finger.

I was in a bay once although the water was green not blue and it was cold and I was lost in it because my Father's arms hadn't reached me yet.

IX

One of a million medieval bright ideas was that the air was made of invisible wings.

It is fairly simple to make your arms into a representation of the crossbar. It is even simpler to close your eyes.

I opened them.

In this section of the Catalogue the leaves beat against the glass, the air is empty, and you are gone.

Sponde, in his love sonnets, writes endlessly on his indefatigable imperative: patience.

But though I lie down, hoping, too often to admit, too often, lately. I am tired.

X

These days, typically, the old projector pours its light, and on the screen there is nothing, so I write to you with my fingers all over the page:

Dear Sweetheart,

Paris is lovely the old labors are finished and I am outside standing in the sun.

1

He smoked one cigarette then another then stubbed out a third because she was back. Back exactly and as quickly as she'd said and now sitting beside him her legs crossed her hands holding the all but empty glass her hand then touching his then going back to the other at the glass then his hand going to rest on her back between the shoulder blades and she turning her head and looking at him not smiling which was better than smiling, he thought, now at this point much better having come to this etc., he thought then thought: and now this and now this and now this.

Just then the waiter came over. The waiter came over in exactly the way he had come to expect all the waiters of Paris forever to approach their customers, which was always seeming to arrive a little ahead of themselves but not hurried even if harried at any rate just always that illusion of solidity of permanence presented by the facts of bone and flesh seeming to catch up with events and this always accomplished this illusion always achieved no matter what the crowd and today there was none.

Would you like another drink, the waiter said.

We'd like another ash tray, she said.

Which was nothing really just something she had said and part of the plan anyway something the waiter had smiled at and responded to nothing a gesture a request and its response and anyway part of it all part of the pattern and now just him thinking about it and too much probably too much always and so yes: shut up, he thought.

Shut up, he said aloud, then nodded and smiled at her letting her know that he had meant it for himself, which was the way they had decided he should do it whenever it came up.

The waiter brought over an ashtray and took away the old one and looked just for a moment at her chest.

The waiter looked at the reflection of your chest in the window while he was picking up the dirty ashtray, he said.

Put your hand back where it was, she said.

She was lovely and he had loved, he thought, to hold his open hand palm flat against the firm bone above and between, he thought, her breasts, firm but light there where the ribs began their spread.

He put his hand on her back between the shoulder blades.

Good, that's good, now look, she said.

Outside the window, exactly in the middle of the slightly yellow reflection of two people at a table one with his arm curved around the back of the other out across the empty street in the trough of the street between the high cold houses an old woman had appeared and was turning slowly rotating dangling a closed umbrella that must have been making the small sound of scraping and then smaller still the sound of her coat in the wind and old feet on the uneven stones and her breathing probably that sound too but muffled by the others definitely muffled by the others definitely.

The old woman stopped turning and went away.

Presently it began raining.

He looked back at her.

She was smiling now and relaxed and smoking a cigarette and he thought: I can look at her chest now and the waiter can look at her chest now and she can look at her chest now and everyone in Paris and it won't matter and what a diseased line of thought anyway.

He nodded and smiled at her which was another part of the code.

Who's crazy nobody's crazy, he thought slipping his thumb up the line of her spine and touching the smooth skin that made a hollow there over the beginning of the heavy, the most significant bones.

She wove her arm up around his slipped her hand up his neck and found the same.

Cranium, she said.

It starts there yes I'm better, he said. I'm better each time.

We agreed we wouldn't say it that way, she said. I already know you're better.

Then, looking carefully at him, she said: would you like to leave or stay.

Stay, he said smiling settling back into the chair.

All right yes stay, he thought. I'd like to stay I'll stay. He reached for a cigarette the room began turning I'll stay forever, he thought, he took his hand off her neck lit the cigarette which was the signal and smiled brightly at her.

I'll be back in a minute, she said.

All right, he said smiling.

I'll come back in a few minutes, she said.

All right.

Goodbye, she said.

Goodbye, goodbye, he said smiling.

2

It starts in a wine bar on the rue Saint Jacques in the 4th Arrondissment. It starts after a single shared glass of red wine, some sandwiches, two cigarettes, and 25 minutes in a crowded room.

It starts.

Then, later, etc., and she put her hands on his shoulders draws her fingers down over his chest then over his waist then around to his lower back.

Etc.

Once upon a time he had long slim arms double jointed at the elbows. He had long slim double jointed arms and large hands and delicately articulated bones around the shoulders. He had delicately articulated bones around the shoulders and smooth skin and long legs wide at the ankles. He had long legs wide at the ankles and large smooth feet and hair that was brown and red and blond and longer than shoulder length and fell across his face at times and the sun coming in though the kitchen window would light it.

Once upon a time she did not have long slim arms double jointed at the elbows and little articulation of the bones around the shoulders although her hands were large and warm and very nice. Her legs were long and gently lined with muscle. Her shoulders were broad especially if viewed from behind and her chest was sweet and pale and her short dark hair was shot around the edges with gray. Her step, too, was worth considering, she moved discreetly, and he wondered, considering her, how someone could move so smoothly she moved through the afternoon light towards him and swept the burning hair from his face.

The top of his arm is in light from the window.

The top of your arm is in light from the window, she says.
It is The Colour of London, she says.
It is the color of A Traveler in Rome.
It is the color of A Traveler in Southern Italy.
It is the color of The Chinese.
It is the color of The Mycenaens and Minoans.
Of The Discovery and Conquest of Mexico.
From the Rio Grande to the Artic.
Of Cairo Vanished and Vanishing.
Of Israel 1988.
Of Australia Today.
It is the color of The American Tourist Manual.
Of Shopping in China.
Of Come With Me To India.
Of African Adventure.
Of Eggplants, Elevators, Etc., she says.

Please shut up now, he says.
Yes.

3

Once, the man asked her what she thought the result would look like if someone succeeded in, say, walking around a circle of zero circumference, and she looked up from her book, glanced around the room, grinned, and said,

And grinned and said,

There was more to it than that of course.

There was more for example when the woman suggested they play hide and seek without the one who was it ever taking his/her eyes off the one who was not.

You first, she said.

The game would end when the one who was it had blinked.

What did you see? said the woman. You, said the man.

The woman went over to hide. The man followed her.

The man went over to hide. The woman followed him.

I see you, he said before the game had even started.

What game? she said.

And vice versa.

By and by their bones began to collide.

(Twenty or thirty centuries passed.)

4

She took another drag off the cigarette and pulled something out of the dark
leather bag she had bought at a market: the market and the purchasing of
the bag being collectively one of the things she had just described to him.
It was a nice bag with two large outside pockets and heavy black pegs for
buttons—exactly the kind they had admired together in an expensive shop
and had been convinced she'd be able to buy cheaply on her trip.
She handed him something.
It's a drum, she said.
It was a drum.
Or a cross between a drum and a rattle it was made of wood and mud and
two pieces of hide was colored blue and red had two wooden balls attatched
to it by short strings and was played by a flicking motion you made with the
forearm and wrist. Inside the drum cavity were some beans or light pebbles
that he could just see when he held it up to the light.
Thank you, he said.
She took another drag off the cigarette and offered it to him. He shook his
head and she put it out.
Thank you, he said again, managing to smile, then taking her hand.
Her hand was cold and he made a joke about it.
Neither of them laughed.
Then she told him some more about the trip including what would have been a
funny story about the enormous woman who had sold her the drum, who had
tried for something like half an hour to tell her in Arabic what the drum was

used for. The enormous woman who had sold it to her had called it a drum something like twenty or thirty times.

Drum, drum, said the young woman, now, here, back again in Paris, pointing at it.

It is a drum, he said, giving it a flick.

It takes practice, she said. You should have heard the woman. If you do it right the gravel gets going.

Ah, said the man.

Practice, he said.

She started another cigarette.

The man looked at his wrist.

The waiter came over then left.

It had been very hot in the desert. Hotter, she had written him (Dear Sweetheart, it is hot), than they had imagined, so she had gone around the whole time with a black hat on her head.

She had been burned anyway fairly badly and you could still see where the skin had peeled.

There was an outdoor shower, she had said.

The waiter brought over another drink.

They looked at him.

He went away.

I want you to tell me. Right now, please, the man said.

5

And the fights even the small furniture flying this then that this yes then no then no then this no or yes no yes.

Nothing was broken nothing and no one the fights went into the bed with them where they weren't where they were no longer fights.

The room was dark. Then dim. She was smoking.
Dream? she asked.
Yes.
Yes, she agreed. There was a bird in your mouth. Or several.

Dear Sweetheart,

Dream in which the little courtyard here was very large and filled with new and used station wagons. Then the world lost its gravity and the cars started floating up to hit against the bird net. No one in the courtyard got hurt but a couple of leaders were transformed into answering machines. The conditions were that the leaders couldn't speak unless someone called. No one could find a phone. So we forgot about them. Cars were bouncing off the net then back up off the ground. Everything was elastic. Things seemed to be accelerating. Not that this matters but I had developed some kind of low power ray beam that I could shoot out of my fingers. A strictly last ditch kind of affair. It only worked about every other time I tried.

6

In 1907 a Navajo woman who had been traveling with Jumpin' Johnny's Wild West Show became interested enough in a French Architect to move into his apartment in the 5th Arrondissment in Paris. An unpleasant situation—'unpleasant' was the way the architect later put it—that lasted three weeks. She left him and got a job cleaning ovens in a small bakery by the Luxembourg Gardens. A year went by. The woman, who did not take another lover, spoke only enough French to clean ovens, and made few friends, fell into the habit, in the early morning after work, of walking through the Gardens. Several men immediately fell in love with her and trailed along individually and collectively carrying flowers. Once, someone spent almost an hour speaking to her in French. No, she said. The man, who told the police he'd done nothing untoward, checked into a hospital, and all the others, when word got around, threw away their bouquets. The woman began wearing a red veil on her walks. Sometimes as she strolled through the rows of chestnuts she would sing. People began to talk about it, and a reporter tried to interview her. The story that appeared near the back of one of the daily papers spoke of 'the woman in the red veil vanishing into the trees.' One Spring morning in 1909 someone took a photograph of her looking up towards one of the statues to the west of the Round Pond. In 1910 she quit her job at the bakery and the walks stopped. People continued to talk about it. Veils of all colors were subsequently found in trash cans all over the Left Bank. The story was changed and included, under the title *The Blue Geisha*, in an anthology of Paris ghost stories. In 1917 a touched-up post card was made of the old photo and sold for a reasonable profit along the quays.

7

He read the newspaper article again. It was a full page spread with three photos of a 12-story building that had been blown—with about 800 people—very nearly in half. The article spoke of children running bloody in the streets. The article spoke of children running bloody in the streets. There was a picture. One of the mothers was quoted. He lit a cigarette. He tried starting over then stopped.

He finished his cigarette hid the newspaper then went over to the bed then re-hid the newspaper then made fresh coffee set the coffee on the table cut slices of bread ate one of the slices set the rest on the table and went back over to the bed.

Then went out.

Rain and cars.

He walked down the street to a flower shop where they made boxes out of rose leaves and lumpy things out of moss and clay. The interesting looking employee he had wanted to talk to for a long time but hadn't wasn't working there any more and the shop was full of people buying lilies. He didn't like lilies but thought of buying one or of trying to steal one thought he would steal one started seriously sneaking towards them then thought not some guy was giving him the eyeball went back outside and bumped into the waiter who worked at the place they always went to.

Hello, he said.

She would like that, he thought, she would like, he thought, that instead of stealing a lily he had run into the waiter.

Hello, the waiter said.

They had a theory about the waiter.

They had several theories about the waiter

All kinds of things.

Once she had seen him in a dream.

Waiterman, they called him.

Waiterman was wearing jeans and a leather jacket and looked almost exactly, here in the rain on the street not in a dream, like everyone else.

He couldn't wait to tell her.

What would he tell her.

He thought about it.

It's an addiction, she would say.

The two of them would lie there, days at a time.

See you later, said Waiterman.

See you later, he said.

Recently she had been to a show where the players had all taken up impossible positions and held them and on her way home she had thrown up. Recently she had shown a clear predilection for talk that centered around people who had shown themselves to care desperately about things. In her dream, Waiterman had been composed largely of pigeon eggs, all but his face, quite lovely. He himself had appeared in her dreams. Once as a sprig of watercress. Once as himself, but somehow horribly. His grandmother had loved lilies. He was not against flowers in fact loved them most of them. He did not have a clear position on watercress. Often he felt horribly. He did not like whipped butter. He liked, even less, plastic tubs. She did not care. On this point she did not care. He had gone swimming once in a deep blue bay and had almost drowned had been drowning I am, he had thought, drowning, because his father's arms hadn't reached him yet. Later they would like the cathedral. Warm stone. Rhythmic mumbling. There was some cure that involved a sapphire. Or a ruby held lightly under the tongue. The Dowager Empress Tz'u-hsi had ingested, each morning, a crushed pearl. That was another country. He wished he had not thought of his grandmother. Standing there. Lilies. Waiterman.

What was he doing in your dream.

Who.

Waiterman.

Being made of eggs.

Besides that.

All kinds of things.

He thought.

It was raining.

And cars.

How was your breakfast, he would ask.

Where is the paper, she would answer.

He walked for a while then. Then wished he'd brought a hat and stopped.

8

It did finally get cold in Paris. No one could deny that. It got clear and cold and the meat carcasses that hung from hooks in the back of the open meat trucks glistened in the light from the yellow street lamps that had started coming on as early as five o'clock. Nothing much besides the meat carcasses was happening in Paris that Fall despite the headlines and the decrease of travelers in the Metro and one young woman one cold November evening went into a café to complain about it.

I know, said the bartender.

It's ridiculous, said the young woman.

I know, said the bartender, who was wiping glasses then filling them with beer then taking them off the counter washing them wiping them then filling them with fresh beer then collecting money where appropriate and putting change into small brightly colored plastic change-plates then thanking the customers who were leaving and saying goodbye to the ones who were walking out the door and hello to the ones who were coming in.

Dear Sweetheart,

We go for a walk along the edge of the world in the evening under all the yellow lamps next to all of the cars, and then no cars, and just the bright building ahead that looks, for a moment, quickly finished, like a burning face.

9

Old Kyoto: city with as many temples as Rome and Paris have marble arches:
city of gardens, rice, and exquisite torture: city of 12 year old Geishas in
silk carrying shamisens and warriors wearing breast plates of bone and
steel: vast city of ancient men and women bent into all manner and angle
of irregularity by calcium deficiency, shuttling along through narrow cedar
lined streets with bamboo canes and scorched oolitic limestones for eyes.
Everyone had heard of the thief. Everyone had seen him.
Seven people including one Samurai and one middle-aged woman claimed,
simultaneously, in different parts of the city, to be the thief, and were boiled,
summarily and simultaneously, alive.
The thief struck again. The boilings multiplied. The entire city turned out in
the evenings and walked along the torch-lit streets.
The thief only robbed temples and shrines.
The thief is a ghost, said the Emperor wearing a heron's mask and 427
people jumped off bridges, slit their throats, or set themselves aflame.
A ghost, said the Emperor.
People drew sutras all over their bodies.
100 priests came out of retirement.
Bells rang and the thief entered a temple dressed as one of the temple
guards.
He reappeared wearing a peasant woman's robes in the pine forest to the
west of the city holding a jeweled sword.
Then went home and had dinner with his wife.
The Emperor, wearing a crow's mask, asked the thief to visit him one evening

at the imperial shrine. A great bronze vat was set on a pile of pine chunks and charcoal on the snow covered ground just outside.

Goodbye, said the thief to his wife.

He came dressed as a 7th century warrior priest. He shook the snow from his shoulders, took off his prayer beads, and laid them at the Emperor's feet. The Emperor laughed, pointed with a long hooked finger to the bronze vat, and the thief jumped inside.

The Emperor laughed.

You have come a long way, he said.

It was market day. The thief was to be executed. A crowd gathered.

The thief's wife and family were found: he had two daughters and a son. The wife and two daughters had their throats cut, and the boy, who still had his milk teeth, was stripped of his tiny robe and tossed into the luke-warm water with the naked old man.

Why are we having a bath, said the boy and the crowd roared.

The old man put his arms around him. He ran a gnarled thumb down the delicate curve of the boy's jaw. The water began to get hot. The old man sang into the tiny ear. The water was hot. The thief whispered something then wrapped his hands around the small boy's throat.

The Emperor and the thief in the bronze cauldron sat staring at each other. Snow covered the ground. Enormous owls flew back and forth through the black air.

Don't leave without first singing, said the Emperor, closing his eyes.

10

She lay down hoping to think but she did not think. She was tired.
The television happened to be on.

Then there was a program about World War II. It was the soldiers who were
now old being interviewed in their salons and offices and clubs. It was the
soldiers with paunches and puffed faces and translucent skin.
The war, they said.
The war the war the war, they said.
One and by one and by one.

The interviews all centered around the question of sleep.
All you want to do in the army is sleep, said an old man sitting behind a
mahogany desk. You never sleep at war, said another, who was sitting in the
center of a beige couch under a painting of himself in uniform, according to
the portrait he had once had thick blond hair. You eat and you march and
if it's snowing you sleep in the snow and if it's raining you sleep in the rain,
said another handsome old man who had been a captain in the infantry
I was a captain in the infantry, he said. There was a close-up shot of the
medals he was wearing. They were blue and green and gold and green and
gold.
Sometimes they slept standing torso to torso.
There was old footage.
Soldiers walking with their heads down.
Soldiers staring at their hands.

An old man staring at his hands.

Two of the men being interviewed cried.

Stop crying, whispered the woman on the couch.

She fell asleep.

When she woke the man was lying beside her.

The television was off.

Music was playing softly, music she didn't know.

I just bought it, said the man.

I don't like it, said the woman.

She woke.

The man was gone and the television was still on. Football players were running a slow multi-colored curve across the screen.

Whoosh, said the man coming into the room carrying a basin. He knelt beside her his jeans were torn at the knee she could see blood there she did not touch it he took off her socks she put her feet in the steaming water.

She woke.

Music was playing music she knew though couldn't name, not ever.

Not liking it, she went to the kitchen and ran a thick stream of hot water while the basin was filling she ate something old she wiped off the counter she turned off the water she blew on the basin and added fragrant salt.

She woke.

He was asleep.

Then he was awake and was watching her.

He was moving his mouth slowly and watching her.

Stop, she said.

SMALL SICKNESSES OF LOVE

He stopped.
Have you eaten, she said.
No, he said.
We have to, she said, eat.

She woke,
It was raining. Waves crashed. They were alone on a great field.
Shall we dance, he said.
Yes, she said.
Shall we sing. Shall we raise our hands in praise. Shall we bow down. Shall we
Most strong God, who is able to fight against you. Shall we batter my heart,
Three person'd God. Shall we good and great God I can not but think of thee.
Shall we how shall I describe Lord the vision of your face. Shall we…

She woke.
He was sitting quite naked beside her.
The death mask of Menelaeus, he whispered. The jewels of Helen. The cross.
The swords. The white pillars. The whips.

She woke.
He stood before her.
Stop crying, she whispered.
Stop stop stop stop, she said.

11

I don't have any way to get the book so I haven't actually read the story or any of the other stories but I've seen a picture of the author and read the review of her book and have read the quoted ending of one of the stories which seems like the kind of story I wish I could write about Paris. I don't have the review right here so I can't tell you what the reviewer wrote to lead up to the quoted ending of the story in question but it makes a lot of sense: it's about a beaver, a female beaver swimming just below the surface of a lake, swimming quickly and below the surface so that she, the unapologetically anthropomorphized beaver, feels, effectively, invisible, safe and shooting into her own constantly shifting equation of *slightly-off-centers*, and yet a clear V is being made by her movement on the lake's otherwise ice-still surface: a smooth-moving analogous index: a V *she isn't aware of*, and this is what is especially beautiful I think, this next move in the review, which is to quote the open ending of the story, something very nearly like this paraphrase: She thinks she is alone, she really does, she is counting on it, *but* the whole lake is pointing at her. Which, I take it, in the context of the remembered review: *my only context*, means, simply: Something very nearly like:

12

A man and woman got onto the train at L'Etoile they were both laughing
there was only one seat left and the man said sit and the woman laughing
said no you sit so he sat and she jumped onto his lap then he said something
and she leaned back and his head disappeared then his arms came slowly
out around her ribs so there was just his legs and all of her and now the dark
hair on his white wrists and the carefully moving fingers and she smiled and
got quiet still laughing but quiet now and the man said something and the
woman said something then the woman looked straight up at the ceiling and
started to scream.

13

We might, said the woman, having just read aloud the invitation to the gallery opening to take place that evening and now sitting at the small round table, we might, she said again, lifting a pencil off the grainy surface then biting into the pencil then putting the pencil back, attempt not to appear too elaborately, she said to the man who had come over to lean in the doorway, to appear, she repeated to buy time for a moment: the man's sudden appearance (she had geared herself and pitched her voice to speak to him through at least two walls) having changed it, even slightly whatever it was (a current end to this current sentence, she thought, etc., etc.)

***

The barber, elegantly huge, had listened with a professional's grace to the man's vague account of that morning's travails.

Travails, is the way he had put it.

It is hard, said the barber.

Yes it is, agreed the man.

Very, sighed the barber.

Indeed, said the man.

I, for my part, said the barber...

Ah, said the man.

I, for my part, said the barber, in galloping off in search of my own humanity, he continued, though pausing for a moment to dip his comb in a jar of blue liquid, have on more than one occasion wished with great desperation to lie myself down, at last, out of doors, in a warm field, on crushed wheat, where I would be bitten, though not savagely, by huge slow-flying insects.

What, said the man.

Yes, said the barber. I have also at the same time registered the immense and apparent idiocy of this.

Whereupon he took one quick monocular scan of the man's outrageously feral mop and told him it would be better for the planet for me and for the lady if the better part of it were to come off.

***

It had come off, and now the man stood shorn, slightly chilled and effectively alone in the basement of the huge converted house. The art spectacle he was now witness to was enhanced both by its basement locale and by the basement's musty smell. (Come look at this, the woman had said before disappearing. At what, he had said.) A tightly packed circular arrangement of light-bulbs, some of them broken, lay on the dirt floor. Above it, trailing a frayed strand of copper wire that spit bits of blue spark when it connected with the aluminum ends of the inert light-bulbs, was a single, sporadically illuminated, sporadically illuminating, low-wattage light-bulb attached to and propelled by a long, slender, slowly moving, mechanical arm.

***

What, he had said again, earlier, before now, though thinking of now, before this, though thinking of her and of insects and of this, this lightbulb, this mechanical arm, above its field of broken lightbulbs, and the people coming to gather around him in the dark and on the street, it was daylight, passing by and he went off to look for her, lately he was always looking for her, sitting in the chair weaving through the crowd with the copper wire spitting blue sparks and the barber moving savagely in the mirror behind him.

14

One of the books I didn't buy recently, but perhaps should have, was about strange things that *could* happen to Paris: a book that had on its cover a heavily varnished painting of three sperm whales swimming over a submerged Arc de Triomphe, and had, as one of its entries, an illustrated description of a plan to elevate the entire Île de la Cité so that roads and channeled water could pass, 'as distantly as dream,' below it.

I bring up that book because it contains images and ideas useful for the following piece, which will—I intend—echo, in its conception at least, that section of Lautréamont's *Maldoror* containing the line, 'My heart, however, is still beating'. Which serves as a pre-echo for the description of a sword blade being shoved down and subsequently lodged against his/its/Maldoror's spine; a section that is —for its heavy reliance on metonymy and synecdoque which permits the one (Maldoror) not so much to slip into but to *begin by* being the other (God)— absolutely, perhaps even etymologically, baroque.

I don't want to push this too much (I hope you will forgive the imminent breakdown of syntax; I will do my best to expediently regroup) but it seems, fairly frequently, and especially this afternoon when I walked over the cold river and across a triangular bed of freshly laid asphalt: then past the elaborate play of waters in the two fountains on the Place de la Concorde: then up the triple column of chestnut trees that compose deep, bench-lined troughs along the north side of the lower half of the Champs Elysees: then up past the Rond

Point with more fountains and beds of multi-colored tulips to the shop-lined, recently renovated and widened half of the Avenue, where thousands of people stroll in a long, wide, rippling spread that leads all the way up to the Arc, the Arc of Triumph, which just sits there—albeit majestically—day after day in a corrugated sea of pigeons, slack-jawed tourists, exhaust fumes, etc. Etc.

It seems… it seems *what?*

I stopped about halfway up the rows of chestnut trees and sat down on one of the green benches.

I was thinking about the asphalt I'd walked over.

Solid but still steaming.

And the last thing I'd read was the section of Saint-Amant's poem, *Moses Saved,* where an outwardly calm, inwardly hysterical Moses parts the 'red' waves and leads a hoard of ferociously joyous people into problematic, because temporary, freedom: across lumps of black coral and still-inhabited crab shells, past streaming walls of salt-hazed water that throws back their crazy, broken reflections, charging their post-migratory dreams of God and redemption with flickering images of kelp forests, wrecked ships, and emerald eyes…

I'm just kind of sitting there on the bench.

Surrounded by kids and couples of all ages, trying, as best I can tell, to vanish into each other.

It looks like it's working.

I imagine it's working.

I get really still.

Then see the room where the two of them are sitting on a hot day like today with the windows and blinds thrown open they are sitting on wicker chairs facing each other breathing hard.

I think that's right. I'm almost sure that's right. I look around.

Cars go by in the distance.

Everyone goes by in the distance.

So.

It's hot in the room and the two of them are just sitting there, staring at each other, trying to decide what? for the millionth, for the billionth time, what? What? And Who?

15

In 1674, a young, well-placed aristocrat, Jacqueline Francoise des Moulins du Bois, fell deeply in love with a young moderately aristocratic, prospective adventurer by the name of Gustave du Camp, who, taking as pledge three emerald rings one tiara two necklaces and several loose diamonds, booked passage and set sail with moderate fanfare for the New World . 'The New World,' du Camp wrote des Moulins du Bois in a letter dated March 19, 1675, 'is a land of Savages and Megaliths.' This brief communiqué, as fortune and circumstance would have it, was the only one that des Moulins du Bois was to receive. In 1680, a mutual acquaintance and co-adventurer of du Camp's described, in tastefully expurgated fashion, the young man's death: 'He was found,' the co-adventurer succinctly described, 'in the snow'. This mutual acquaintance, who wore a two-fingered glove on his left hand and high collars to cover his neck, thereupon returned to the moved but not overly grief-stricken young woman the three emerald rings one tiara two necklaces and several loose diamonds, that had been, as he put it, retrieved. Des Moulins du Bois, who subsequently became des Moulins-Beaufort, afterwards received some small recognition at court for having been among the first to create and experiment with a very nearly viable design for a diving suit, and for having been found, one Spring morning, as her very much bereaved husband put it, 'in the well.'

16

Once upon a time when they were walking together, they saw a man selling oranges in the metro and decided, later, that it might be important for at least one of them to remember that once upon a time when they had walked together, hand in hand, they had seen a man selling oranges in the metro, in case they decided , later, that it might have been important to have done so, together, to have done or seen something together, once.

17

The following document was recovered from a crumbling 1907 pamphlet entitled, somewhat enigmatically, Life is Stranger Than Truth, Volume II: Nine More Miniature Gods.

"On the 15th of September, 1840, at 6:01 a.m., a certain Jean Biche woke to the news that his uncle, in dying, had named him the sole heir of a considerable fortune, and at 8:01 a.m. that same morning he took possession of the now defunct uncle's Paris mansion and began very slowly to bash out its interior floors and walls, a process that took him several years. When the several years were over and the enormous house stood gutted, monsieur Biche, or the Marquis Sans-Tête, as he was afterwards known, boarded up and hermetically sealed all the windows, purchased the entire living inventory of the teeming local bird market, released it into the vast dark space, sprinkled the brim of his hat with bird seed, and stepped inside."

Dear Sweetheart.

Dream in which Paris becomes a tropical rainforest complete with sloths blowpipes toucans flying monkeys and flesh-devouring diseases. In this new Paris the umbrella-hat salesmen and their suppliers get rich and when you go into the Café de la Mairie you sit on moss seats and watch the people paddle by. Everyone sweats. Everyone who moves too quickly catches a disease and dies. I have a good anti-disease gimmick. The gimmick is I get engaged to a sloth. The wedding is set for the end of the tree branch which gives us plenty of time to watch it all happening around us. It all happens around us. After a couple of weeks it's pretty much just parakeets and enormous flies.

18

Cette descouverte d'un païs infini semble ester de consideration

Man:

This afternoon as I was coming home I walked through a grounded flock of pigeons there were crumbs covering the sidewalk and the bed of dead roses they were bunched thick and barely moved engendering on my part a more than somewhat gingerly propagated (and curiously accordion-like) advance so I halted and for a moment stood still then saw the butcher he waved I couldn't just stand there up to my ankles in pigeons with the butcher waving at me. He had on his apron it was covered with as much color as usual I do not know what or if any of this might adumbrate the butcher's wife was standing behind him in the shop I didn't see her fingers or their dog but thought I heard it as I passed. I went into the spice shop and stood looking at the cheeses for five minutes all the shop men moved around me I could smell their surfaces finally I decided and left. It was the same with the fish and canned vegetables I chose trout and pickles finally I made it out of the store and came home. You were not here so I sat at the window. While I was waiting I unwrapped one of the pieces of cheese broke off some of it tasted was not satisfied so unwrapped the other piece of cheese followed the same procedure was satisfied this time and was still satisfying myself with that second piece of cheese when the old woman from upstairs appeared in the courtyard. She wore a grey skirt black shoes thick grey stockings that sagged slightly at the ankles and a blue

cardigan sweater buttoned twice. She stopped in the middle of the courtyard
pulled a piece of tissue from a pocket I couldn't see blew her nose so softly
I couldn't hear then stood up very straight and the sun fell smack on her
white hair and I thought of the Eiffel Tower it was once a docking station for
dirigibles. I looked away for a moment and —if there is a point to any of this
it is this—when I looked for her again she was gone.

Woman:

I sat in the third row as usual it was quiet at first they came and went around me then I was tired of sitting so I got up and went with them we made beautiful ovals around the bays. There were candles burning in the chapels. Some of the chapels were closed. When I was tired of walking I went back to the third row and sat down. Two priests walked by they were both holding gold boxes carved with stars and crosses then another priest walked by holding a book. All these priests wore white. They walked along the south passage past the columns. They kept vanishing then reappearing. There were windows behind them the words "they were lines that lived on color" came into my head. The chairs in front of me were almost empty there was a bald man in the second row and three nuns kneeling in the first. Above and to the left of the nuns was the row of receding King Windows and above the bald man who was sitting unusually straight-backed with his hands placed together high in front of him was the North Rose. Then I closed my eyes because I was tired of looking and when I closed my eyes someone in one of the chapels to the East began to sing. When I opened my eyes the singing didn't stop. I could not tell where it came from. Camera flashes were going so I looked up at the walls. The light was coming in through the South Rose and colors and pieces of color lay across the stone. The singing stopped. Someone pointed. I saw but could not reconcile what I had heard with what I could see: old men coming out of black iron gates. They spoke in Latin. They sang. It was not the same singing. The cameras kept flashing. Everything had become different so I stood. Outside—and here is my point—it was Paris. I walked quickly. As I was coming home after-images of entire windows smashed into everyone I passed.

Dear Sweetheart,

The knight meets the furled lady. He desires her. She desires to elaborate on his lineage so unfurls and advances through the green groves merrily until they meet. They meet. Then the son arrives and they all dance a carole that breaks into farandole they all dance a moonlit carole that unfurls into a merry farandole until someone dies unto dieu and then they all through the green groves sadly retreat.

19

Le Vair Palefroi

Li palefrois s'en va la voie
De la quele ne se desvoie,
Quar maintes foiz i ot este,
Et en yver et en este.

I

A young man with a beautiful horse is in love with a young woman who lives near the center of a forest behind a high, circular wall. The wall has cracks in it. The young man rides his beautiful horse as close as he can to one of them. I can see you, the young woman says. Yes, the young man says. No, says the young woman's Father, who is very old and very rich. The young man starts to leave, sad. Even if you are not rich your Uncle is rich and friends with my Father, suggests the young woman as the young man is riding away. He rides away. Uncle, he says, you are rich and I love the young woman and you are friends with her Father. How much do you love the young woman, asks the Uncle. As much as the bird the bough and the bough the tree, says the young man. What does the tree love, asks the Uncle. The wind, says the young man. What does the wind love, asks the Uncle. Nothing, says the young man. The

50

Uncle nods. I will do what I can, he says. The young man leaves on his horse for a tournament, happy.

II

The Uncle and the Father are very old. Once they were young and jousted in the forests and fought with swords in the fields. Once it was morning in the Middle Ages and they wore young women's sleeves on their glittering armor and galloped against each other. How they galloped. We are young, they said. Now they were old, but did not say it. Listen to what I say, said the Father. The young woman tore at her clothes and ran from the room.

III

The young man won the tournament and went home on his horse to his house. He was very happy and very young. The Father and the Uncle arranged the wedding. They were very old and all their friends were old. There were no old women in the forest. They had all gone off to live in the West. What, said the young man. We need your horse for the wedding, said the rider who had appeared at the young man's door. We need your horse for the wedding so that the beautiful young woman will have a beautiful horse. What wedding, said the young man tearing at his hair which was long and lovely in the morning wind. But the young man was a young knight so the rider on his horse and the morning wind on the young man's beautiful horse rode away. The young man tore at his hair. He told his servants that if they sang that evening or any evening ever he would kill them.

IV

Then it was night. The wedding was to occur in a ruined chapel just as dawn became day. It was night but the moon was full and all the old men who were to escort the young woman to the wedding became confused because they thought it was dawn and that the wedding in the ruined chapel was to occur in just a few moments when it was day. So they saddled their horses. They put the beautiful young woman on the young man's beautiful horse, but the young man wasn't there.

V

Through the forest they rode. All the old men. And the young woman. And some of the old men spoke and some of the old men slept. We are old she is young, some of them said. Some of them slept. The young woman did not sleep. The moonlight was very bright and the forest was very silver. The forest was very silver and the beautiful horse was gold and silver and turquoise and black and finally the young woman slept. She slept. Then she woke and was alone on the horse and was riding down a silver path through the silver woods. I am scared, she thought. Beautiful horse I am scared, she said. The horse walked. He could not talk. He walked.

VI

The old men were still sleeping and talking and moving through the trees. They arrived at the ruined chapel and wondered about the dawn. We were wrong, they thought, the birds were not singing it was night. We were wrong and now the young woman is gone and now birds are singing so it is day. It was day. The beautiful horse walked over a bridge near the young man's house.

Who is there, said the bridge keeper. I am, said the young woman. The old men were riding through the forest. Soon they were lost. They galloped. They had been knights once but now they were lost. The old men galloped. Hello, said the young man. I am here, said the young woman. I can see you, said the young man.

VII

It was day now and the forest was no longer silver and the Uncle stood waiting in the ruined chapel: he was waiting. The Father was not waiting. He was asleep. He was dreaming. In the dream it was raining in the West and the old old woman smiled. Then he woke and went away.

20

The apartment gave onto a small courtyard and was surrounded by houses and narrow streets. It was evening and raining and mist was rising. The courtyard was dark with rain and the floors in the apartment were smooth tile or thick carpet and you could move over them without making a sound. The woman moved over them without making a sound.

Then went out the door and into the rain.

Despite the rain and the rising mist the streets were crowded and she walked with and against the crowd quickly then slowly then quickly again. The stores along the streets were still open and people came and went through the yellow doorways and people stood peering into the yellow rain-streaked windows and dripping lights were strung through the trees. Three men spoke to her from under the glistening surfaces of umbrellas and when the fourth one turned towards her she stopped waited until he was close enough then pushed up his umbrella and screamed. Then was gone into the crowd across the avenue down three short curved streets looking behind her then not looking behind her then down a long dark slanted road to the river and onto a bridge. She went over and leaned against the stone railing. She looked down at the water. She looked again. She separated a piece of wet hair from her face. She pulled the long piece of hair straight inspected the ends then pulled it over into her mouth and chewed.

A man approached.

He went away.

A tourist boat came down the river, spraying the mist yellow with its lights, dimly illuminating the grey buildings, the high walls, the dark banks. Gulls came after it, silently wheeling, dozens of them, their white breast feathers catching then losing the rain and mist-shattered lights, all of them vanishing together when the boat went under the bridge.

The woman jumped off the bridge.

The woman stood on the bridge.

Something.

Dear Sweetheart,

I go to see a famous ventriloquist who is having cardboard children, sitting cross legged in a circle, tell ghost stories. Every few minutes all but one of the cardboard kids cough. Then I cough. Then I am sitting down next to the ventriloquist on the ventriloquist's bed. Watch, I say. Only I know I haven't actually said anything because I don't know what it is we're going to watch. Then the lights dim. And there are only candles and a few coals in the fireplace. Watch, I say again. I watch. Glowing in the shadows, sitting opposite each other, are a chimera and a sphinx. Cute, I say to the ventriloquist. Then I realize that I am the ventriloquist. Cut that out, I make myself say. I am myself again. Then I am the ventriloquist. This repeats until I'm confused about who is saying what. I said that, says a voice. No, I did. Then the sphinx says, stop. And now I am sitting opposite the sphinx. Hello, says the sphinx. What do you want, sphinx, I say. I want an answer, says the sphinx. To what. To the riddle. That's an old one. It's a new one. So what is it. I realize my lips aren't moving. I am watching the sphinx and the chimera. We are talking. We are sitting in the center of a huge stage. A wind rattles across us. We are made of cardboard. We glow. My lips don't move. Neither do theirs. I tell the riddle. I listen to the riddle. I answer it. There are only three of us now.

21

It had been a very heavy man and they were forced—the presiding doctor commented on this—to use scalpels with blades nearly twice the normal size. They cut a flap through the skin that had covered the lower ribs and stomach and pulled it neatly down over the groin. This man died of cancer, said the doctor, holding up a length of intestine in his left hand and pointing at something, something imperceptible about it, with his right. The assistants continued working. They had made preliminary incisions along the arms and now were doing the same with the hands. They drew the scalpels across the wrist. The doctor turned back towards them still holding the length of brown intestine. Then he looked up over the corpse towards the observers and said something else. Everyone was taking notes. The lights in the room were very bright so that the doctor could not look directly at them. There was a camera filming the procedure and part of the time the doctor addressed it. This, he said. That, he said. He used a black fountain pen to point. The assistants were now working on the head. They pulled the face down over the jaw and cleared away the fat deposits that had gathered against the bone. They used a kind of suction tube then a soft wire brush. Then they used a saw. The doctor named the pieces. He described the functions. Everyone was taking notes and making sketches. He removed one of the eyes. He held it carefully between his thumb and index finger while one of the assistants clipped something with a pair of bright scissors. Everything around the body shone. The doctor looked upwards. He was talking into a microphone connected to the camera. He spoke clearly and slowly. Everything was in Latin. The assistants stopped for a moment to listen. Then they went to work on the shoulders. Everything was shining. The doctor kept talking. Someone repeated very softly what had just been said:

Iam dies alibi erat illic nox omnibvs noctibvs nigrior densiorqve. Vbi dies redditvs is ab eo qvem novissime viderat tertivs corpus inventvm integrvm inlaesvm opertvmqve vt fverat indvtvs habitvs corporis qviescenti qvam defvncto similior…

22

Until recently, in the early morning, it was still possible to enter the city of
Atget and to feel underfoot the carefully swept gravel of its gardens, to stroll
in the ever more certain shade of its trees, and to peer, in passing, into the
pleasantly darkened windows of its boutiques and bottle sellers and cafes,
where occasionally one would discover, perhaps set fast in the center of one's
own reflection, a pair of eyes, a forehead, a pale frozen hand. Even then,
when almost everyone had gone inside, or had gone still, or had been caught
in motion and so, as it occurred, had vanished or almost, it was still possible
to encounter the occasional blindered horse or sleeping dog or small
gathering of people, the men in their hats, the woman in their high-waisted
skirts. One didn't dare salute them, however, for fear that in the relatively
precipitous movement of their reciprocation they would disappear: once,
I offered a lump of sugar to a horse whose head, in accepting it, vanished;
on another occasion, I startled a boy who giggled and became a pale blur.
No one can say for certain what will become of Atget; some contend that
one day the dust motes caught in its icicles of air and light will begin to
shiver again and to turn; others believe that with the passage of years Atget
will begin to crack and then to crumble; still others that Atget will remain,
impervious, while the world around it melts and reforms, melts again and
fades. What is clear is that when it became common knowledge that Atget
was freezing, there were many who left as quickly as possible; and as many
or more who rushed in. One of these last, wandering bewitched, I left Atget
without knowing it; when, realizing, I turned to go back, it was no longer
possible to get in.

23

Absolutely not, agreed the man. In fact that might almost, said the woman, as they were leaving the theater and heading off now, slowly hurrying off now, along one of the dark cobbled streets, into a low breeze, so that a pleasant or pleasing sense of friction, etc., I completely, said one or the other of them, as they walked and walked, and the eyes, the eyes of the occasional people they passed.

Dear Sweetheart,

A 'dance' implies a gathering of bodies in space. A gathering of dancing bodies implies a collective though perhaps tacit awareness of the presence of space in the mind. I ask the pale gentlemen who has been telling me this when exactly the music is supposed to start please it's getting late. He winks and tells me that the ongoing presence of ghosts in one's dreams implies an ongoing and exponential exchange of space for body and of something for time. What do you mean by something? I say. Nothing, he says. Which makes the walls and floor and ceiling vanish, so that the hall is no longer a hall is no longer anything and everything that begins to happen around me and then inside me and then instead of me is shot through with stars.

24

The Tour Saint Jacques rises beautifully into the sky across the Seine from the Saint Chapelle where for hundreds of years kings were served mass by candelabra under the high blue star-scorched groin-vaults at the west end of an extremely dense field of impossibly lovely stained glass windows some of which are now—the originals—on display in a museum in the 5th Arrondissment that costs 35 francs to enter unless you happen to know someone which they did.

They went in through a small gate off the main courtyard that led straight down into the old partially excavated gallo-roman baths where huge coffins, funereal stones, and chipped 14th century statues are kept.

They have concerts there on Wednesdays.

What.

That guy we met who works there said they are supposed to have concerts there on Wednesdays around 6:00.

Then it was Wednesday. They went into the enormous stone hall and took a seat in the back.

Really, said the woman.

It was Tuesday again and they were standing at the counter of the café trying to drink the coffee because they were both for the first time that week trying not to drink anything else.

Well, said the man.

Well, let's go, said the woman which they did the next evening it was four old men giving a creaky rendition of some small work by Bach.

Fuck this, the man said a few minutes later, still Tuesday, he started to order a drink but the woman touched his hand.

She ordered the drinks.

She ordered two more.

They sat down.

They got dignified.

It's Bach, he said.

That's pronounced, 'Baak'.

I know it is.

I know you know it is.

They looked at each other. They grinned.

Let's go, she said, meaning in or out the door, any door, either Tuesday or Wednesday or Friday, whichever.

It was Paris.

Look, they said.

They bought strawberry crepes at a stand near the Pont Neuf then kissed perfunctorily then groped at each other then laughed and kissed seriously then walked along the river towards home.

25

It is when, in its final pages, the book begins to treat of what it calls 'the extended field of speculation' surrounding Maître Francois de Montcorbier dit Villon's 'disappearance'' that it becomes interesting. The first postulation is attributed to one Alfret de Mainz, a 16th century barber/surgeon and sometime chronicler who asserts in his *Notes on Fair Devious Knaves* that Villon went not as he had forseen he would, i.e., 'dying upright in the light' on the much feared gibbet of Montfaucon, but dying upright in the dark, in a cow shed just outside the city walls, victim, de Mainz maintains, of some dubious, but finally *definitive* justice at the hands of two or three slandered creditors, one of whom was said to have been a judge. Jean Alloue, 122 years later, writes, we are informed, of an unnamed author who claims to have discovered a crumbling letter rife with uninhibited invective against perceived incursions by 'les genz du nord,' which makes passing reference to 'that poet-thief broken into bitter stanzas on the wheel.' The letter in question purportedly bears the seal of one of the members of the landed Gentry whose estates lie just to the north and east of Dijon, that city of a thousand spires which Villon, with verisimilitude, can be imagined to have admired. The book then leaps into the 18th century where we find, variously, Villon being burned, badly bled, drowned, stoned ('like an Arab'), and quartered ('like a Jew'). One *Belle Plume* confections up an account of Villon being fed to death with hot apples! The same author, in a variant account, attributes the gourmand poet's demise to poisoned plums. Most convincing, perhaps (or most compelling, at least), of the book's confabulations are the final two. In the first we find Villon, though publicly condemned to exile, privately condemned to much grimmer desserts: clapped in irons, he is led back to Meung sur Loire**, where, with his arms locked behind his back, after being lowered by ropes into that watery dark, he is thrown a fistful of gold coins and told that, should he grow hungry in the days to come, he can ingest that. The second, built on the first, exceeds even the absurd. It supposes that Villon is once again extricated from the abominable fosse***. Once freed, and stopping in Strasbourg before crossing the Rhine for 'one last gulp of dark red wine,' he makes his way slowly East then slowly South, so that four years after that last dark drink, we find him negotiating for passage to the 'land of spice and dragons' with the leader of a caravan in the Holy Land. Three years later he has 'seen what Polo saw first before him' and has had sharpened bamboo applied to his fingers and gums for insolence, rape and theft, only escaping death 'by excision' by being purchased as a curiosity for a Mongolian menagerie. The book then relates that it was part of his ever more improbable fate to watch the sun fade over the inner kingdom from behind the black teak bars of a cage set atop the southern heights of the Great Wall. Here the account takes on the trapping of dream. By a series of impossible events, Villon, now bondservant to a Korean trader, finds himself taking the waters in a hot spring associated with one of the minor temples in Kyoto, Japan. Then—no explanation offered—we find Villon freed of his engagement, fluent in Japanese, and, somehow cosmetically altered, at large in a city the private contents of which find themselves incrementally becoming his own. Suddenly, our hero has a wife. And then children. In between 'acquisitions' he composes Haiku. Haiku that is, by local standard, considered somewhat over-touched by emotion, though not without merit; in fact, 200 years later a poet whose brush will be named for a tree growing outside his small house will, the account assures us, remark on their 'crimson lucidity.' Years pass. Villon's powers as a thief increase. The entire city is made aware of them. The account has transformed the greatest western poet of the late Middle Ages into a

Japanese sorcerer. Sensing an anomaly, the Emperor intervenes. It snows.
Bells toll across temple courtyards. A bronze caldron filled with melted
snow from off the roof of the Emperor's winter residence is set up. Huge
owls come out of nowhere and beat their wings. In the last lines, as the city
gathers, Villon's family is rounded up. The ending is entrusted to drama. A
fire is lit under the cauldron. Villon's hands tighten. There is a monologue
involving masks, and a boiling ensues.

(Endnotes)

* In 1463, Villon, sentenced to 10 years exile, vanishes from the record.

** Villon spent the summer of 1461 in this dungeon of dungeons.

*** Villon was freed from his initial incarceration for having written during
that incarceration a poem strung well enough to please the ear of no less a
personage than Charles D Orléans.

26

Tell me one of your dreams, said the man.

All right, said the woman. In the afternoons I would walk down the street in company with one or two others, friends or otherwise, and at the end of these walks there was always a game.

What kind of game.

A game with ropes a game with sticks a game with colors a game with balls a game with paper a game with stone glass coin opal ruby a game where we joined with others and built fortresses or raced across a field or ran across the ice and fell.

Other times I would walk across the apartment and peer into my parents' room and I could see their outline in the bed the covers of white and their combined shape rose out of the rounded flatness of the huge bed and the shape of their breathing rose higher still that was in the early morning when I was small and it was Summer outside and I was just up off my bed so that when I looked at them I was not at all sure that what I was looking at was them (a dilemma compounded by the fact that both slept with a pillow over their head) so I would count the number of breaths they took, watching the covers rise and fall, and in so counting, very often, as I remember it, would suddenly find myself back in bed.

In the evenings I walked with my father we walked along the canal at dusk the ducks swam by he told me to keep my eyes peeled we might see a goose or a swan he told me the tale of the swan then the tale, I think, of the crow and once he told me that our country would win the war what war I said and he said there is no war never mind.

One morning I walked into the kitchen and my mother had just painted the ears of one of the dogs the brown one Dougal the black one Dillon was barking in the closet my father wearing a bright fresh rose did not return until the following afternoon.

Tell me one of your dreams, said the man, drifting.
I have just done so, said the woman. Good night.

27

the wide terraqueous world....
-Herman Melville

I

W: In a small room with two chairs two small tables two small lamps two small books set off from each other by a certain distance.

M: Dark surrounds except perhaps for a small high window or two low windows with the blinds drawn lit for a moment each and each after the other before going dark. Occasionally there are blinking multi-colored Christmas lights.

W: Man and Woman enter and are seated.

M: Ahhh...

W: Ahhh...

W: I was under the bridge. You know the bridge with the earth ground into the stones and the general arching effect. And one or two huddled masses. Under the supports. And on the river for once there were actually boats.

M: On the river.

W: Smothering the river.

M: What kind of boats.

W: Big boats. Small boats. Row boats. Sloops. Triple masters. Junks. P.T. Boats. Aircraft carriers. Dinghies. Pleasure ships.

M: Proceed.

W: Anyways and etc. there I was with the 13th century Our Lady in sight
and a corner of the 19th century Prefecture in view and seeing out from
under the 18th century curve of the bridge towards the other bridge and
you know how it smells under the bridge and the sounds and the sea gulls
and the pigeons and the people passing and the huddled masses under the
supports and the boats smothering the river and it was snowing…

M: It wasn't snowing.

W: No. No you're right it wasn't snowing, and anyway it was snowing and
kneeling at the grave next to me were two girls with bows in their hair hands
held together faces down one not quite down so I could see her pretty chin.
There was a wall behind them and a tombstone covered with names and
the snow falling silently on the graveyard and the man coming along in the
tractor with all the leaves piled up behind.

M: Which way were you facing.

W: The grave.

M: Proceed.

W: The streets were flooded or folded I forget which which year that was we
went along in long low boats and didn't trail our hands in the water for fear
of having our fingers bitten off by rats although we did look at ourselves in
the waist deep water there being no fear that our reflections might be bitten.

M: Did you leave the flooded streets and set out onto the flooded river.

W: You couldn't. I forget why. It would have been very nice yes but there
was something about concern for the safety of the great fish and you couldn't.

M: Yes I remember now. About the safety of the great fish. It concerned
their dorsal fins. Quite…delicate. Proceed.

W: This is just a little bit. A wee bit. A small pale boy in a yard in front of a
pillar and a brick wall and a window and a vine or shrub and the wee bit of a
boy's bright white feet are angled left and his white face is angled right.

M: That's already more than a little.

W: It is. It's true. They… grow.

M: Into…

W: Never.

M: No.

W: What kind of…

M: I don't think I know yet.

W: No you wouldn't. I mean a dog. The kind I mean with the short coat and long curly hair.

M: Long coat but short curly hair.

W: Yes, it comes in through the window sheet after glowing sheet. And the drinks were already set out. Ice cubes and small portions of everything.

M: Poodle.

W: It was a poodle. Yes. Basking in the sun on the stone floor. You know how those floors are cold. Always.

M: I do.

W: Even with a carpet.

M: I do.

W: I'm done.

II

W: Which is lit only by the blue Christmas lights. Only.

M: On the yellow jacket cover you'd put a bit of blue over one of B's eyes.

W: A blue bee eye.

M: Yes. That is the introduction. Enter the players.

W: Clop clop clop. They are entered.

M: In walking. In the city. Not in the moon and trunks and leaves. But there was a moon. It came through a mist of rain or a rain of mist. Something slight. A slight interference only. Because you could still see it, the moon.

W: Above the stoplights.

M: And the headlights.

W: And the shoplights.

M: The moon. The moon much like a something. A something glow-in-the-dark.

W: What it does.

M: Glows.

W: In the dark.

M:

W: Or in the light.

M: You'd put a bit of blue over one of Baudelaire's eyes.

W: Yes.

M:

W:

M: And the shoplights. Once as a boy I went into a cellar with another boy the boy whose cellar it was had a glow-in-the-dark skeleton doll I shrieked, then laughed, then they started talking in the dark around me, older voices, terrible voices, I was 8 years old.

W: How many were in the cellar with you.

M: Thousands.

W: But the moon.

M: Thousands. In the light. I think it is in the light that it glows.

W: Curious.

M: A curious mist of rain in which I met a man carrying flowers and a woman carrying bags and an orange cat and a man on a bicycle with a chain around his waist and

W: Curious.

M: Curious what. I was walking. I met them. It rained. A small girl stood with her doll in a pram in the snow.

W: I think it is in the dark that it glows.

M: Not possible.

W: But still. But still yes I too went into a cellar with another when we were children only in this cellar what we had set about to see were the glowing hands of a watch that had been taken from the top drawer of a parent's dresser and held under a lamp. And then we were in the dark having descended stairs and my friend said look and I looked first at her voice then heard the light ticking tick tick tick and looked at the watch.

M: And shrieked.

W: Yes but later.

M: In the dark.

W: In the light.

M: Oh.

III

W: Once on my way to S. I met a woman who led me into a ditch.

M: Just like that.

W: There we were.

M: Was it a wet ditch.

W: Not entirely, though the earth at the base of the long grass blades was dark and cool.

M: How did you know it was dark.

W: We lay there. We were lying there. We lay in the ditch the day long and the day was long then I bade her farewell.

M: I love you.

W: Yes. It was I after all who covered one of Baudelaire's eyes with a bit of blue. But the ditch.

M: The ditch.

W: The ditch. Did you know that it is recorded of some people, among them Alexander the Great, that their sweat exhaled a sweet odor. Did you further know that Helioglabus, the Emperor, once harnessed two stags to his chariot and after that four dogs and after that four naked girls, being drawn by them in state, he also naked. I mention these things because as I lay there in the ditch rubbing my eyes, an action which usually engendered an explosion of stars and exclamation points, what I saw forming were fine lines, clear lines, that after a moment became arches and temples and even aqueducts.

M: In the ditch.

W: Yes.

M: Curious.

W: Yes. I lay there a while afterwards and along comes an old woman this time who tells me she's lost her shoe.

M: Where has the other one gone.

W: It's on her foot. I check. There it is.

M: I meant…

W: The other. I'm with you. She is disappearing off in the distance. She is dark against the white gravel of the road.

M: And the surrounding hills. Were they white.

W: The hills were green. No, they were purple. No, blue.

M: Blue hills.

W: This was in Kentucky. I asked the old woman what she thought she had done with it. The shoe. She said she thought she had given it to the cats. Initially. But had discovered, subsequently, that this supposition had been wrong.

M:

W: Because the dog had long ago done away with the cats and so the cats were long gone.

M: That's pretty sad.

W: Yes it is.

M: And then she too was gone.

W: Reduced to residuum.

M: Went limping off.

W: Before I could help her.

M: Or even think to.

W: The old biddy.

M: In the…

W: Yes.

M: And this after the…

W: Yes…

M: Of the other one.

W: Once upon a time upon my way to S. I met an old man with a truck load of pig manure. He was on his way over to what he called his other farm.

M: He offered you a ride.

W: Upon the pig shit.

M: And you…

W: Yes. Once after all I had ridden on top of a truck load of salted cod from maybe Zaire to Rwanda I think. And this being involved in the pig shit was for but a little way along the road.

M: In Kan Tuk Eee.

W: And then over the river into Indiana where the hills are decidedly not blue.

M: They aren't blue in Kentucky either.

W: In a mist they are blue.

M: And Indiana.

W: Was mistless. By this time I was walking again. That territory has for its base the finest oolitic limestone. The mines are vast and the woods deep and all the time you keep stumbling, depending, to some degree, upon the season, into corn. Do you know corn? It's a perfect plant.

M: Perfect in what way.

W: Perfect for sun perfect for rain. In Indiana you might almost say they worship it.

M:

W: In one corn field however the owner had constructed a maze, based, he told me, on the divine maze at Chartres, and was charging a nickel for the fun of negotiating it.

M: Five cents.

W: Yes.

M: That isn't much.

W: No it's not. I gave him one on my way out.

M: And the woman. The younger one.

W: Still disappearing. Off at the horizon.

M: And the older one. The one who had misplaced her cats.

W: Her shoe. Forever lost. Limping off. Into residuum.

M: How did you know the earth in the ditch was dark.

W: We lay there. We dug in it. You should have seen our fingertips. The earth in the ditches in that part of Kentucky is full of worms.

M: What was the pig manure man's name.

W: Farmer. He looked like a tall turnip.

M: What about the maze.

W: It was tall, too. Taller than your head and dried because it was early October late afternoon so the sun came smashing through it and as you walked dry leaves smacked against your face and there were children in boots with bright faces and even when you couldn't see them you could hear them and there were crickets and crows and we ran and the ground was hard and shone in places like polished stone.

M: And then.

W: And then nothing.

M:

W:

M: Exuent.

W: Return and bow.

28

One morning, nearly finished, she looked over across the room and saw him sitting there with his eyes open, not moving much, thinking. Occasionally he moved. He would lift an arm or his jaw would do this thing or he would reposition his head. A fly went skittering along the wall: he kept not moving, thinking, presumably thinking. What are you doing, she asked. He told her. In detail. It was not particularly interesting this thinking, and then he was back at it, sitting there, as many fat slow flies in the room as you like and he wouldn't care, or wouldn't move, the stinker, did you notice the fly, she asked, no, he said, or, perhaps it's more like I wouldn't care, she thought as she looked at the sheer hard hull of his skull and imagined the electricity in there and the dampness. Thought, she thought, is electricity. That moves through dampness. Cold and wet or warm and wet. Cold and wet. And I think there is a certain magnetism involved. Or is that involved with memory, which is certainly, nonetheless, however, involved with thought, she thought, he is seeing things while he is sitting there with only his jaw and nose twitching and sometimes a leg and that is electricity and that is dampness and that is magnetism. Houdini was a thinker. Houdini was also a stinker and a sinker as they would as they were known to tie him in chains and toss him into lakes not warm lakes lying there at the bottom in chains he was gone he wasn't sitting there any longer no longer and she thought ah here it is the distinguished dampness and the magnetism and the cold cells hanging clustered having come through corridors upon corridors or coils upon coils perhaps accompanied by a low cold clicking, no, she said, no what, he said from the other room. It was sunny, Sunday, and it went on.

29

It was this old man about four and a half feet tall, or whatever, in a brown leather jacket and blue baseball cap, and he was having trouble pulling luggage up over the curb so I helped him, and he thanked me, then when he saw I hadn't left immediately he said: BACK OFF!

Fair enough.

Luckily I saw the old guy again about fifteen minutes later and this time he was sitting on a bench with his feet propped up on his luggage smoking a cigar.

Want a cigar, he said.

No, I said.

He was a funny old guy and looked pleasantly ridiculous all bent up on the lamp-lit bench. He was actually pretty good looking. Dark eyes. Fairly straight fingers.

How old are you, I said.

98.

98 years old this guy was and out on the street with luggage at 2:00 a.m.

What are you doing, I said.

Which he didn't tell me right away because he then asked me if I had any change.

No, I said.

Just thought I'd try it out.

I looked at him.

What a weirdo.

Then he said this:

What are you doing.

I'm hustling, I said.

You're hustling.

Yes.

Doing any good.

No.

Ever do any good.

No.

Want a cigar.

No, I said.

Then he said:

I'm visiting Paris.

I looked at him.

I've just started. Now. Tonight. I live near here.

He pointed sort of up into the air with the cigar.

I sat down.

Yeah, I said.

He fished around in his pocket and pulled out a picture of an old woman
kind of sagging into a couch. He said a few things about the picture: when it
had been taken, etc.

I looked at him.

I'm just seeing the town. Thought I'd take off for awhile. We thought I should
start tonight. So here I am.

So here you are, I said.

There was so much cigar smoke you could barely tell.

I mean that he was crying.

But he was.

I'm just out visiting Paris, he said.

You said that, I said.

I know.

He said some more about his wife who apparently liked to stay up reading late.

So I shook his hand.

There was nothing special about the handshake.

She's probably reading right now, he said.

It was just two hands.

And I don't care how many bones that is.

Or about the oxygen content of marrow or how rapidly with the passage of time it depletes.

I looked at him.

We shook hands.

It was beautiful.

It was like pulling cool silverware from a dishwasher.

He said something about his fish tank.

I knew what he meant.

I know what you mean, I said.

And walked off.

I went back over to the café and straight away scored a hit with a woman in her late forties good looking good legs good perfume.

You look good, I said.

You look good, she said.

Etc.

Actually, I went home.

I just came home because I'm thirsty, I said.

Yeah, she said.

30

It was as likely a place as another for a ghost to visit, it had always seemed to me, so that when one night one did visit, or, rather, appear, I was not quite as surprised as I might otherwise have been had it not, as I have said, always seemed so, so likely, so to speak.

It was late at night, granted.

He, not the ghost, was asleep.

He was asleep and I was awake and it was late.

Very much.

I was a reader of ghost stories as a child, were you.

In those stories there were always branches scraping at the windows and little boys and little girls stuck into cracks in walls and the wind blowing across them and strange sad lights in the distance and moors to traverse and old quarries and all manner of faith and devotion betrayed and weeping always weeping and persons wronged.

I remember one in which a traveler alone was forced by circumstance and poverty to sleep, night after night, in a soaking-wet bed. A bed bone-dry by dawn. Or the one in which figured the ghost of a whipping boy. The maid in the corridor. The queen with the head in her hands.

Recently I read about a man who once, perhaps in hopes of provoking the periphery of the paranormal, or perhaps only of proving a theory, the account wasn't clear, burned a rose and waited all night for its ghost to appear. You will see, he had been instructed, the palest shimmering.

It was late, I say, and he was asleep and then I was asleep in my chair in the other room and then I woke and she was sitting very straight in a chair not quite opposite me.

Very clear.

Uh, hello, I said.

Hello, said the ghost.

One is not, in one's life, granted very many interviews with ghosts, so I stood up, crossed the room, and shook her hand.

It was warm and small and very much shakable.

I held it a moment.

You are a ghost, aren't you, I said.

Yes.

So that was that. I let go of her hand.

She was a very pretty this ghost. Very lovely. All curves and fine coloring.

I told her so.

She thanked me.

There was a silence.

Can I get you something, I said.

No thank you, she said.

Not a drink?

No.

A snack.

No thank you.

There is some meat in the refrigerator.

What kind of meat.

I'm not sure. Meat. It's cold.

Well, no thanks.

We sat there.

She was nice to look at.

You're sure you're a ghost, I said.

Absolutely, she said.

Why can't I see through you.

I don't know. I can't see through you either.

She smiled. Gorgeous teeth.

Oh, I said.

It was actually very pleasant. To be sitting there. Conversing. Extremely.

You're very pretty, I said.

Yes, thank you, you've already said that, she said.

But she was. I mean enough to say it twice.

I heard him turning softly in the other room.

That too was pleasant. The sound of his turning. The sound of his quite

warm flesh, his quite earthly constituents. He moans sometimes. Very softly.

In his sleep.

We sat there.

Well so what's it like, I said.

Being a ghost.

Yes.

It's grand.

Really.

Yes.

Not too lonely.

No.

Never lonely.

No, no not really, there are a lot of us.

That made sense.

I see, I said. And what are you all doing.

Doing.

Yes.

Well, we don't really do anything.

Just sort of float around.

Not even float around.

And you're all right with that.

Yes.

I see. So you're just over visiting.

We call it appearing. We don't visit people we don't know. We appear. If it's a relative then we call it visiting.

And do you ever visit yourselves.

I don't understand.

I didn't either.

So what you do is you appear.

Yes.

Then she disappeared.

Or vanished.

Or whatever.

Too bad.

It was still of course, very late, and he was still, of course, asleep, and if he was moaning or turning he was moaning or turning too softly to be heard, and then I was asleep and then awake again, but not very awake, because it seemed to me I saw, across the room near where my ghost had sat, a pale shimmering, much like a pale white rose, although I do not know what color rose it was the man in the aforementioned anecdote had burned.

I burned a preying mantis once.

Doused it with engine oil and lit it.

Wow.

But it was a pale white rose I saw shimmering as I sat there, late at night, not a mantis burning, probably more than half asleep it seems likely, while he lay fully asleep in the other room.

Salome was pale. In the play. As pale as the reflection in a silver plate of a white rose, it goes.

Bring me the head of the Baptist!

Or something.

A drink.

Scoot over, I said.

What, he said.

Or, peradventure...

You're back, I said.

You bet, she said.

I would like, at times, to be as pale.

31

"Not in the morning because in the morning it can relieve them of the necessity of having to choose not between but because of the most that they can state by the time that it is not thought of as relief to it if by any chance he and she were to come together and state that the time which was more than enough to have to have as if it could be ascertained that they arrange the rest of it in the meantime as believing left to them with an alteration of their arrangement with soothing and left to it mostly as an elevation of their allowance which must be strange as they are inclined to have it very nearly as much in an allowance of their pressing as if when left to them they try to be not very much with and behind in the part of the arrangement which cannot force them to be patient as long as there is more in the place of their arrangement and closing it to them as much as if it were partly only playfully left to be dangerous to an inundating plan of their having oceans of intervals and mostly as they liked."

—Gertrude Stein

32

The Petit Fer a Cheval is a wine bar on a long narrow cobbled street that marks the western edge of the Marais in Paris. Fer a cheval means horseshoe. There is a bar in the front room of the Petit Fer a Cheval that is shaped like one, and around its counter there are always customers, standing or sitting. In the evening almost all the customers are young, well dressed, even very well dressed. Some of them are well dressed in leather some of them in suits. The bartenders who mix the drinks and smoke always are tall moonlight as models and flirt with all the customers: more openly with the woman more genuinely with the men. There is also a waiter—very efficient—who comes and goes through the smoke.

The back room of the Petit Fer a Cheval is larger than the front and not as smoky. There are tables there where people can eat. Not just the standard very quickly familiar café food but full meals. Veal, salmon, rabbit, calamari. The waiter is willing and very much able to help you select an appropriate wine. Everybody selects an appropriate wine

A couple, or almost a couple, a pair of young people who look very much like they are about to become a couple, two people who keep kind of, etc., are sitting at one of the tables in the back room. There are many other people in the room eating and drinking, drinking and eating.

So.

The young woman says something has another drink of wine then puts her finger in her mouth reaches across the table and touches the young man between the eyes. She touches him again. The young man is grinning. The wine is very good and very cheap. The young man grins. Maybe, he thinks. He doesn't want to look. He looks. The waiter comes over with their salad. Everyone is talking. The waiter goes away. The young man puts his hands on his silverware. Then in his glass. The young woman says something. She says it again. He touches her —The End—and drops of wine run down his cheek.

32

A gorgeous sun was shining on Paris. It was lovely. The wind was blowing in the trees. There were leaves on the trees. Everything was very lovely. A crowd had gathered around the woman. They all craned their necks to look up the side of the bright building. They all craned their necks as the woman pointed. An old woman in the crowd kept trying to touch the young woman but there were too many people. I can see it, said the old woman. Her hands kept creeping forward. There were leaves on the trees. Everything was very lovely. The leaves, because it was spring time, were a brilliant green, and the wind blew through them making the trees come alive. The old man who was with the old woman looked like he might fall over if forced to hold his position much longer. He did not however fall over. The young woman did. By and by a young man helped her up. Along the street the stores were open, and men and women went into them then went back out. It was clearly an arrangement. The men and women went in then came back out. This repeated itself. It was like a carnival. Or a something. Or a something or a parade.

Later they went to the Museum of Comparative Anatomy next to the Jardin Des Plantes where the sun was also shining, perhaps even more brilliantly because there were so many flowers to see. Inside the museum among the bones and bottled organs it was dim and warm and there were funny little birds flying back and forth under the ceiling lamps casting quick shadows on the bottled organs and bones. It was quite an extensive collection though everything seemed either too large or too small or too large and too small and after about 15 minutes they felt dizzy and walked out.

Outside it was lovely. They walked down the shady lanes and up the sunny rows. The man hummed. The woman smiled. Pigeons flew by. An old couple was feeding them. The sun made patterns on the warm swept earth.
And presently the woman started pointing again. The old couple looked up then came over. A crowd gathered. The young man made himself ready. I can see it, said the old woman. They all stood looking at the sky.

Dear Sweetheart,

Democritus said there was neither up nor down in the infinite void,
and compared the movements of atoms in the soul to that of motes in a
sunbeam where there is no wind. Max Ernst said that Perturbation, the
hundred headless woman, is living alone on her phantom globe, beautiful
and dressed in her dreams, and that her smile of fire will fall on the
mountain sides in the form of black jelly and white rust. Gertrude Stein said,
climb up in sight climb in the whole utter needles and a guess a whole guess
is hanging. Hanging hanging. And you said, whatever the truth of the world
it was simple: they were speaking about milk.

PARIS: AN AFTERWORD

One day though, and someone comes along, picks the matchstick up, and presses it against the striker, rubs its poor, dear, good, little head against that striker until that same little head weeps fire…

1. For many years this book was not a book (it was a dream, a figment, a highly enervating folly).

2. Then it became a book, one that was almost immediately, like the character who sets off unprepared through the woods, very hard to find.

3. I wrote the draft of what would eventually become these pages in the Fall, Winter, and Spring of 1994/1995 in Paris when I was studying French Modern Letters at Paris IV (La Sorbonne). I sat at a round table and smoked and drank coffee and/or wine. Instead of being a good or even reasonably diligent student, everything I read for school I turned into something I was reading for writing. When I sat reading Jean Giono (*Noé, Un Roi sans divertissement*) in the courtyard of the Sorbonne drinking bad espresso from a plastic cup I was writing. And smoking. I had this deal with myself that the first cigarette of the day had to wait until I was in that courtyard, with that plastic cup.

4. I smoked a great deal in those days. And wandered. Constantly. This wandering was mainly about being able to stop — on street corners, in neighborhood cafes, next to flower vendors, on swept gravel paths, under plane trees, outside movie theaters, under the eaves of churches, next to garbage bins, beneath stinking bridges, etc. — and smoke. Smoking, you saw things. Smoking, people came up to you and asked you for a light.

5. Books are bones.

6. This book is bones (fundament, residue of some initial, wayward impulse). Bones now getting to rattle again. It is also smoke. You suck it into your lungs. It relaxes you. It makes you choke.

7. You is I. (I has always been someone else.) Bones get burned.

8. I quit smoking, more than once, some years later in New York.

9. Someone once remarked that they liked the book but why was everyone always smoking? Someone else said why another book about Paris? Not a book about Paris, I said. Not *about*.

10. It was very hard for me to stop writing these stories. I would go out, wander (smoke), then come back and write. Repeat. Also I would read (it bears repeating) a lot. In many of the books I read (e.g. Montaigne, Gertrude Stein, Jean de Sponde) there was a great deal of wandering (if not smoking) going on. I would read then I would write. I became highly permeable. A sheet of thin, perforated plastic. The world peered in through me. I peered in. What did I see?

11. I composed almost entirely on a first- or second-generation Mac Powerbook. Every few stories, I had to take the trackball out and scrape it clean. Ash having entered. Flecks of food, tiny globs of jam.

12. One day my screen went out and I was too broke to get it fixed. For weeks I worked by shining a desk lamp on it and looking at it from the side. I got headaches. Neck aches. Carpal tunnel. The poet Stephen Rodefer showed up on my doorstep with a portable typewriter he had carried across Paris. So I could keep working. Rodefer, a.k.a Jean Calais, being the author of the marvelous *Villon,* whose influence can be felt in these pages.

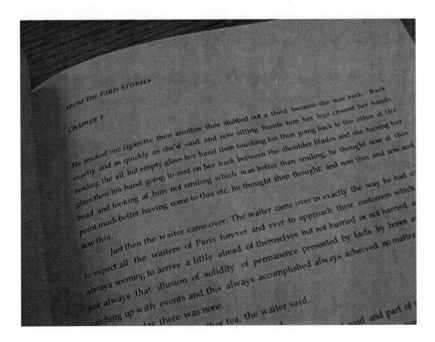

13. This was not the first full-length book I wrote (there was another involving checkers, dwarves and velvet dresses in a closet). But it was the first full-length book I published. For a time, in manuscript, it was full of photos. A diver deep below the sea staring up to the surface. A field of tulips swamping a windmill. Rowboats drifting through flooded Paris. Things drowning/drowned.

14. In *Lavish Absence: Recalling and Rereading Edmond Jabès*, Rosmarie Waldrop, an early reader of *The Paris Stories*, writes, "I choose to sit in the café Danton that serves its sugar cubes wrapped in portraits of Rimbaud or Proust over the café that serves the history of the *gendarmerie*. Who wouldn't. When I saw Edmond Jabès for the last time, the sugar came wrapped in the French Revolution." There is everything and nothing in this: Paris. Everything carries the day, but nothing is there too.

15. *Dear Sweetheart, Democritus said there was neither up nor down in the infinite void, and compared the movements of atoms in the soul to that of motes in a sunbeam where there is no wind.*

16. Exactly.

17. In the first or second volume of his epic, unfinished *2666*, Roberto Bolaño has a man hang a book from a clothesline in his backyard. It hangs there for days, weeks. I don't remember if it eventually falls or just fades away. In this book I tried to hang myself from a clothesline slung across some enormous Parisian courtyard.

18. I learned how to write stories by trying to write poems after having read many poems. Whose poems ("May was a cavernous month/A thing sweeter than yam")?

19. When we visit Paris now we take our daughter. She plays in sandboxes. She runs giddy, screaming. Across the swept gravel. Up the tree-lined avenues. There is good candy to be had in Paris. Good candy and many fine pastries.

20. Which is to say that on a sunny day in Paris you can (still) observe shadows engaged in all shape and variety of exotica. Not to mention chatty old men with fingers that feel like cool silverware sitting with their feet propped up on suitcases.

21. And that I associate (still), rightly or wrongly, my impending dissolution, with the dissolution, in my body, of time.

22.

Boulder 2010